The Boys of Paul Street and the Castle's Secret

Elderson Luciano Mezzomo

M617o Mezzomo, Elderson Luciano

The Boys of Paul Street and the Castle's Secret / Elderson Luciano Mezzomo. - 1st ed. - Marburg, Germany : [the author], 2023. - 74 p. : ill.

ISBN 9798856181677

1. Children's literature. 2. Adventure. 3. Mystery. I. Title.

CDD 823.93

Copyright © 2023 Elderson Luciano Mezzomo
All rights reserved.

Summary

Introduction	5
Chapter 1: The Strange Find	9
Chapter 2: The Discovery of the Tunnel	13
Chapter 3: The Encounter with the Redshirts	15
Chapter 4: The Boys' Escape	19
Chapter 5: The Magic Forest	23
Chapter 6: The Ghost Castle	27
Chapter 7: The Lost Treasure	31
Chapter 8: The Unexpected Rescue	35
Chapter 9: The Story of the Castle	39
Chapter 10: The Boys' Mission	43
Chapter 11: The Attack of the Redshirts	47
Chapter 12: Gereb's Betrayal	49
Chapter 13: The Death of István	51
Chapter 14: The Boys' Escape	53
Chapter 15: The Tunnel Collapse	55
Chapter 16: The Search for an Exit	57
Chapter 17: The Temporary Alliance	61
Chapter 18: The Light at the End of the Tunnel	65
Chapter 19: The Final Surprise	67
Chapter 20: The Return to the Grund	71

Introduction

In the pulsating heart of Budapest, there's a small green corner known as the grund. This space has witnessed many fervent battles and fun games between the brave boys of the Paul Street Gang and their arch-enemies, the Redshirts. This was the backdrop of our beloved "The Paul Street Boys," a tale of courage, loyalty, and friendship.

The original book, brilliantly penned by Ferenc Molnár, captured the essence of childhood and camaraderie. The exploits of the Paul Street Boys were fun and adventurous, but also reflected the profound values of comradeship, teamwork, and integrity.

The Paul Street Gang, led by the sharp and fearless Boka, along with his loyal companions, defended their territory with burning passion. The rivalry with the Redshirts, led by the cunning and ambitious Feri Áts, oscillated between friendly encounters and heated battles. Both factions, however, shared a deep love for this piece of land they called home.

The book ended with the boys vowing to protect the grund, whatever it took, ensuring that future generations could enjoy the same joys and challenges they had experienced. It was a bittersweet farewell, leaving readers with a sense of hope and a yearning for more.

Now, dear readers, we find ourselves once again on the brink of that sacred land, ready to dive into a new adventure. The book you're about to read, "The Boys of Paul Street and the Castle's Secret," is a continuation of our beloved story, bringing new challenges and adventures for our intrepid heroes.

This book takes us back to the heart of the grund, where the Paul Street Boys make a discovery that will alter the course of their lives forever. A long-hidden secret beneath the ground of their cherished grund is revealed, opening a portal to a bygone era, an ancient fortress, and a legendary treasure.

However, our brave boys are not the only ones aware of this secret. The ever-lurking Redshirts also uncover the existence of the mysterious tunnel and treasure. A race ensues between the old rivals, each trying to reach the treasure before the other.

The dangers are greater, the stakes are higher, and the stage is set for an adventure like no other. The cast of characters we know and love is back, with new faces joining them, and old allies revealing themselves as traitors.

And as always, the story is imbued with the spirit of Hungary, with its rich tapestry of history, culture, and folklore serving as the backdrop for the plot. Every twist and turn of the story not only brings the boys closer to the treasure but also delves deeper into the heart of Hungarian identity.

However, dear reader, make no mistake. This is not just a tale of adventure and treasure hunting. "The Boys of Paul Street and the Castle's Secret" is a story of growth, learning, and overcoming.

Our heroes face moral dilemmas, make painful sacrifices, and learn valuable lessons. They discover that true wealth is not found in piles of gold or jewels, but in the relationships we build and the values we uphold.

With "The Boys of Paul Street and the Castle's Secret," I hope that you, the reader, are transported once again into the world of Boka and his friends. May you delight in their adventures, feel their struggles, share their victories and defeats, and above all, feel the unbreakable friendship and indomitable spirit that characterize the Paul Street Boys.

So, open the book and join us in this new adventure. The grund is calling, and the treasure awaits. Get ready to laugh, cry, cheer, and be surprised as we unravel the Castle's Secret together.

And remember, just as the grund belongs to the Paul Street Boys, this story now belongs to you too.

Chapter 1: The Strange Find

It was an ordinary summer morning in the playground. The boys of Paulo Street had gathered for another day of games and laughter. Boka, the unquestionable leader, was busy organizing the day's games while the other boys eagerly prepared.

They ran, played, fought, and laughed, filling the playground with the energy and enthusiasm that were their trademarks. The sun's glow struck the green grass, creating an almost magical atmosphere.

Suddenly, Nemecsek, the smallest boy but with a big heart, stumbled upon something hard in the middle of the playground. He got up, dusted off the dirt, and looked at the object he had tripped over. It was a metal cap, partially buried in the ground.

Nemecsek called the other boys, pointing to the metal cap. Boka approached, bent over, and carefully examined the cap. The cap was covered in dirt and rust, but it seemed to be firmly attached to the ground.

All the boys' interest was piqued. They gathered around the cap, exchanging guesses about what could be hidden underneath. Some thought it was an old weapon hideout, others imagined it could be a secret passage to the king's palace.

Boka, the most pragmatic among them, decided that the best way to find out what was underneath was to open the cap. He called Geréb, the strongest boy in the group, to help him lift the cap.

Geréb, with an effort that made his veins bulge, managed to lift the heavy cap. To everyone's surprise, there was a stone staircase that descended into darkness.

The boys glanced at each other, excitement shining in their eyes. This was much better than any game they could have invented. A real adventure awaited them in the depths of the earth.

Boka, always the leader, decided that they should explore the tunnel. He ordered them to get lanterns and ropes, to ensure they could descend safely and find their way back.

The boys, excited about the adventure that was looming, ran to their houses to get the necessary items. They quickly returned, eager to unravel the mystery of the tunnel.

The light from the lanterns flickered on the damp and cold tunnel walls, creating dancing shadows. The descent seemed endless, but the boys' excitement propelled them forward.

Until they reached the end of the dark, dusty staircase. The tunnel stretched out before them, the end hidden in darkness. The boys glanced at each other, knowing they were about to enter the unknown.

Boka took the first step, closely followed by Geréb and the other boys. The tunnel was narrow and low, and they had to walk hunched over.

The sounds of the playground and the city above disappeared, replaced by the oppressive silence of the tunnel. The only sound was the echo of the boys' footsteps and the occasional drip of water.

They walked for what seemed like an eternity. The air in the tunnel was damp and cold, and they could feel the earth beneath their feet. Each step took them deeper into the bowels of the earth.

Finally, the tunnel opened up to a large underground chamber. The boys stopped, amazed by the size of the cavern.

The ceiling was so high that the lanterns barely reached, and the walls stretched in all directions. In the center of the chamber, there was a fork, with two tunnels leading in different directions.

Boka, after considering the options, decided to follow the tunnel to the left. The boys, trusting their leader, followed without question.

They continued their journey, the lanterns' light illuminating the path ahead. The feeling of being in an unknown place, the excitement of discovering something new, filled each of them with a sense of joy and anticipation.

What began as another ordinary day in the playground turned into an extraordinary adventure. And so, the Asphalt Society launched headfirst into their greatest adventure, completely oblivious to what fate had in store for them.

Chapter 2: The Discovery of the Tunnel

They ventured into the chosen tunnel, with Boka in the lead holding the lantern that penetrated the darkness. Csomor, who was right behind Boka, held a rope tied around his waist, the other end of which was secured at the top of the stairs, ensuring they would find their way back.

The damp air of the tunnel and the muffled sounds of footsteps echoing off the stone walls gave the place a mysterious atmosphere, which simultaneously frightened and fascinated the boys.

More and more, they felt like pioneering explorers, discovering a new underground world. The fear and anxiety they felt descending the stairs had now transformed into adrenaline and excitement.

After a time that felt like an eternity in the silent darkness, they noticed a curve in the tunnel. Boka raised the lantern and illuminated the path. The light revealed another fork. Another decision to be made.

Boka looked back, where the anxious eyes of the boys watched him. He knew he had to make a choice. He decided to follow the tunnel to the right. None of them contested. Trusting Boka's leadership, they followed him down the chosen path.

The tunnel seemed to narrow more and more, and they had to proceed single file. The silence was only interrupted by the muffled sounds of their footsteps and the occasional dripping of water from the tunnel ceiling.

The atmosphere changed as they delved deeper. The air became fresher, and an earthy aroma filled their nostrils. Something about the tunnel's environment made the boys feel strangely at home, as if they were returning to a place they had long forgotten.

Then Boka suddenly stopped. The other boys almost collided with him. He lifted the lantern and lit something up ahead. The light revealed the end of the tunnel.

The boys crowded around Boka, looking at what the lantern light illuminated. The tunnel ended in a large, old wooden door, firmly closed.

Everyone's eyes widened in surprise. The existence of this door, at the end of this secret tunnel, was beyond anything they could have imagined.

For a moment, everyone was silent, contemplating the door. Then, Boka stepped forward, with the determination of a true leader, and pushed the door. It groaned and creaked, but finally gave way.

The boys held their breath as Boka slowly opened the door. What could be beyond it? They were about to find out.

Chapter 3: The Encounter with the Redshirts

As soon as the door creaked open, the boys of the Asphalt Society were flooded by an incandescent light that danced in strange patterns on the tunnel walls. The atmosphere seemed heavy, filled with an odd energy, making the air almost palpable.

Nemelszky closed his eyes for a moment, shielding them from the bright light. When he opened them again, he saw something that made his heart race. There, ahead, in the illuminated vastness of the tunnel, were the Redshirts. They too had discovered the tunnel's secret.

The leader of the Redshirts, Feri Áts, was standing, holding a faded map. He spoke fervently, pointing to something on the map, while the others looked on with interest.

The boys of the Asphalt Society retreated, hiding behind the open door. Boka signaled for everyone to remain silent. He sneaked a bit closer to hear what Feri Áts was saying.

The conversation was muffled, but Boka managed to catch a few words. "Fortress... treasure... power... kings..." The words poured out like fragments of a mysterious puzzle, a puzzle that had everything to do with the secret of the tunnel.

Boka felt his pulse quicken. What did these words mean? What treasure was this? And what did Feri Áts plan to do with it? One thing was certain - the Redshirts knew more than they did about the tunnel's secret.

He turned to the others, his eyes wide. He didn't need to say anything. The boys of the Asphalt Society understood immediately. The look on their faces turned from shock to determination.

The boys of the Asphalt Society were brave. They weren't afraid of the Redshirts. But they knew that at this moment, they needed strategy, not brute force.

Boka whispered a quick plan. Nemelszky and Csomor would stay behind and watch the Redshirts. Boka, along with the others, would return to the grund to prepare a proper plan.

Without a word, the boys split up. Boka, Pásztor, and the rest ran back through the tunnel, their hearts pounding in their chests, adrenaline fueling their run.

The Redshirts were still distracted, arguing amongst themselves, unaware that they were being watched. Nemelszky and Csomor shrank further into the darkness, keeping their eyes fixed on the rivals.

On the way back, Boka couldn't stop thinking about the words he heard Feri Áts say. His heart was heavy with the understanding that the secret of the tunnel was bigger and more complex than they ever imagined.

Back at the grund, the boys of the Asphalt Society gathered in a circle, faces serious and looks determined. Boka repeated the words he heard from the Redshirts. The boys' eyes widened at the information.

The news that the Redshirts had also discovered the tunnel and that they had a map shocked them. The mention of a treasure and a fortress lit a fire in their eyes.

The boys spent the rest of the day and most of the night planning. They strategized, discussed possibilities, and above all, reaffirmed their unity and commitment to each other.

They were united in their mission to unravel the secret of the tunnel and, if possible, find the treasure before the Redshirts. The fight was just beginning, and the boys of the Asphalt Society were more than ready to face it.

Boka watched the boys, a smile of determination on his face. He was ready to lead his team into the most exciting adventure of their lives.

Chapter 4: The Boys' Escape

The daylight had already turned into the darkness of the night when the boys from the Asphalt Society met again in the tunnel. They had spent the day planning, preparing themselves to confront the Redshirts. Each one's heart pounded with anticipation and nervousness.

Boka was the last to enter the tunnel, taking a final look at the deserted and silent street. Then, with a deep sigh, he turned and followed his friends into the darkness.

The boys moved silently, communicating only with gestures. Each step seemed to resonate in the tunnel, accentuated by the distant echo. The tension was palpable, an almost physical presence in the darkness.

They arrived at the spot where they had last seen the Redshirts. Boka signaled, and everyone stopped, listening. The familiar voice of Feri Áts reached them, faint but clearly discernible. He was still there.

The boys exchanged nervous glances. Boka signaled them to retreat. The Redshirts were too close, and any noise could alert them.

But, to the boys' misfortune, the Redshirts had already noticed something. Feri Áts let out a cry of alert, and the sound of hurried footsteps echoed through the tunnel. The Redshirts were closing in.

Boka wasted no time. He waved to the boys, and they ran, the sounds of pursuit growing behind them.

The race through the tunnel was a disorienting experience. The darkness swallowing them, adrenaline humming in their ears, the constant feeling of being chased... It was like a nightmare they couldn't wake up from.

But they didn't stop. They couldn't stop. They knew that safety, or at least a chance to escape, was ahead. They just needed to keep the pace and not look back.

The sound of the Redshirts seemed to be getting more distant, but Boka knew they couldn't afford to relax. They needed to get out of the tunnel and find a hiding place.

And then, light. A distant opening, faint, but unmistakably the tunnel exit. Boka pointed, and they ran with renewed determination.

The boys emerged from the tunnel, panting and exhausted, but relieved. They had escaped the Redshirts - for now.

The place they found themselves in was a forest, dense and unknown. It was a completely different setting from the familiar grund and the known streets of Budapest. But it was their hideout for now.

Boka took one last look at the tunnel, now just a dark opening at the base of a hill. The Redshirts hadn't yet emerged. They were safe.

For now.

They retreated further into the forest, looking for a place to rest and catch their breath. The escape had been draining, and everyone was exhausted.

Boka found a sheltered spot among the trees, and they settled there, trying to catch their breath and regain some sense of normalcy. The adrenaline began to fade, giving way to overwhelming tiredness.

Finally, they all fell asleep, wrapped in the silence and darkness of the forest.

The boys from the Asphalt Society had escaped the Redshirts. They had faced danger and overcome it, at least for now.

But the adventure was far from over. The unknown forest, the hidden treasure, the mission to defend the legacy of the ancient kings of Hungary... all that still awaited them.

And the boys were ready to face any challenge.

Because they were the Asphalt Society, the defenders of the grund. They were friends, comrades, a family.

And nothing could stop them.

Chapter 5: The Magic Forest

The boys woke up with the sun rising. There was something magical about the morning light filtering through the leaves, transforming the forest into a world of shadows and mysteries. For the boys of the Asphalt Society, it was like waking up in a dream.

They got up, stretching their aching muscles. Fatigue still weighed on them, but the new day brought new hopes. Boka looked around, trying to assess the place where they were.

The forest was dense and wild, filled with strange sounds and vibrant colors. It was a place unlike anything they knew. Yet, they didn't feel afraid. On the contrary, they were curious.

Boka decided that they should explore the forest. Perhaps they would find a way back to the grund. The other boys agreed, and they set off.

They walked for hours, discovering more and more about the strange place. There were giant trees, exotic flowers, and insects none of them had ever seen before. The bird songs were different, as were the noises that came from deep within the forest.

They found out that the forest seemed to have a life of its own. The plants moved as if they were alive, and sometimes, they had the impression they were being watched. But the boys weren't scared. They were fascinated.

They kept exploring, delving deeper into the forest. Despite its vastness and the feeling they were lost, they didn't feel fear. They were together, and that was all that mattered.

Hours passed, but they found no sign of the grund or any familiar path. Instead, they seemed to delve deeper and deeper into the enchanted forest.

Boka decided they should camp right there, at least for that night. Maybe the morning would bring a new perspective and new ideas. The others agreed, and they set up a camp.

The night in the forest was unlike anything they had ever experienced. The sounds were louder, more intense. The darkness was deeper, almost palpable. But again, they weren't afraid.

They huddled together, listening to the sounds of the forest. Each noise was a new discovery, each shadow a new adventure.

They fell asleep under the tree canopy, wrapped in the song of the crickets and the whisper of the wind. The magic forest embraced them in its heart, its mysteries still intact.

The dawn brought new discoveries, new mysteries. The boys woke up, eager to explore more, to find out more about the magic forest.

And so, the Asphalt Society continued its adventure. They explored, discovered, and marveled. The magic forest became their new world, their new grund.

Because even lost, even far from home, they were still the boys from the Asphalt Society. They were still friends, comrades, a family.

And nothing could stop them. No matter how many mysteries the forest held, how many dangers it hid. They were together, and that was all that mattered.

So, as the sun rose in the sky, they set off for another day of exploration. The magic forest awaited them, its secrets eager to be discovered.

And the boys from the Asphalt Society were ready to discover them.

Chapter 6: The Ghost Castle

After three days of relentless walking, a strange silhouette finally appeared on the horizon: a castle. It was a stone monster, with pointed towers rising above the trees, its grandeur challenging the blue sky. The boys stopped, staring at the castle with awe and a whisper of fear.

Boka turned to the others. "Let's go," he said, and there were no arguments. They moved on, their hearts pounding with the expectation of finding an answer to their troubles or a new adventure.

They climbed a steep hill and reached the castle entrance. The wooden doors were peeling and aged by time, but they seemed solid and intact. They pushed them open and found a large empty courtyard, with stone walls and an unsettling silence.

They crossed the courtyard and entered the castle. Inside, the silence was even deeper, as if the castle was a forgotten place, abandoned by time. Daylight entered through cracks in the windows, creating a ghostly atmosphere.

They roamed the castle corridors, admiring the ancient tapestries that still hung on the walls, the stone fireplaces, and the dust-covered furniture. Everything seemed to have been left as it was, as if its inhabitants had suddenly disappeared.

Boka led the boys to a large dining room, with a long table and high chairs. The room was cold and empty, but they sat in the chairs, feeling small and out of place.

They explored further, climbing a spiral staircase that led to higher towers. Up there, they had a view of the entire forest, a green vastness extending as far as the eye could see. None of them spoke, each absorbing the view in their own way.

Night came, and they decided to stay. They found empty rooms with straw beds and settled down for the night. The castle seemed even more haunted at night, with shadows dancing on the walls and howling winds in the towers.

Despite the eerie surroundings, the boys managed to fall asleep, their dreams filled with images of kings and queens, battles and banquets. Deep down, they knew they were in a special place, a place with stories to tell.

They woke up with the sun rising, the golden light seeping through the windows and illuminating the castle's interior. It was as if the castle was waking up with them, its silence being broken by the sounds of the morning.

Boka got up, stretched, and looked at the others. He had a determined expression on his face. "Let's find out what this castle is hiding," he said, and the other boys nodded, ready for another day of adventures.

They explored the castle for another day, finding more rooms, more corridors, more stairs. Each discovery led to another, and with each passing hour, they felt they were getting closer to something, to some hidden secret.

And then, as the afternoon was almost ending, they found it. In a room hidden behind a bookshelf, they found a treasure. Coins, jewels, weapons, art objects. A treasure fit for a king.

The boys looked at each other, their eyes shining with the discovery. They had no words to describe what they were feeling. It was a mix of awe, joy, and fear.

They started to touch the objects, their fingers sliding over the gold coins, the glittering jewels, the ancient weapons. They couldn't believe what they were seeing, what they had discovered.

But then, something happened. Boka picked up a sword and, as he pulled it from the sheath, triggered a trap. The room's door closed, and the ceiling started to descend.

The boys looked around, panic setting in on their faces. They were trapped, and the ceiling was descending rapidly. They looked at each other, knowing they had to find a way out.

But no matter how hard they tried, they couldn't. The door was locked, and the ceiling was descending faster and faster. They began to scream, to call for help.

But nobody responded. The castle remained silent, as if it were watching their futile efforts. And the boys, trapped in the treasure room, knew they were alone.

Then, when the ceiling was almost touching their heads, an old man appeared. He opened the door with a key, and the boys ran out, relieved and scared.

The old man introduced himself as István, the castle's guardian. He said the boys were chosen to inherit the legacy of the ancient kings of Hungary. And with that, the adventure of the boys from the Bitumen Society in the ghost castle was just beginning.

Chapter 7: The Lost Treasure

The Tar Society Boys stared in disbelief at István, the old castle guardian. They were sweaty, dirty, and incredibly relieved to have escaped from the trap in the treasure room. But what the old man had said had left them even more surprised. To inherit the legacy of the ancient kings of Hungary? What did that mean?

István took them to a different room, away from the immediate danger of the trap they had activated. It was a cozy room, with a large fireplace and comfortable armchairs. They sat, still trying to comprehend what was happening.

The old man began to tell a story. A story about kings and queens, battles and betrayals. A story about a lost treasure that belonged to the ancient kings of Hungary. A treasure that was now in the hands of the Tar Society Boys.

The story was fascinating, but also daunting. The boys looked at each other, unsure what to think. They were just children, after all. How could they handle a royal treasure?

Boka, always the leader, was the first to speak. "We can do this," he said, looking into István's eyes. "We can take care of this treasure." The other boys nodded, their respect for Boka clear in their eyes.

István smiled. "I knew you could," he said. "You are brave and determined. You are worthy of being the treasure's guardians."

With this statement, István took them back to the treasure room. This time, they were careful, avoiding touching anything that might activate another trap. They looked at the treasure with new eyes, no longer as boys, but as guardians of an important heritage.

They spent days learning from István. He taught them about the history of the treasure, about the significance of each piece. He taught them to take care of the treasure, to keep everything safe. They listened attentively, absorbing every word, every lesson.

The responsibility was great, but the boys accepted it willingly. They knew they were doing something important, something that would have a significant impact on their lives and on Hungary's history.

And so, the Tar Society Boys became the guardians of the lost treasure of the ancient kings of Hungary. They began to live in the castle, taking care of the treasure, and learning more about their country's history.

But even with all the responsibility, they were still boys. They played, laughed, explored the castle and the surrounding forest. They had adventures, as they always had. After all, they were the Tar Society Boys. They were adventurers.

Time passed, and the boys grew up. They became teenagers, and then men. They became guardians of the treasure, and then kings. They became legends.

But, even after all these years, they never forgot where they came from. They never forgot their roots, their adventures, their childhood. They always remembered being the Tar Society Boys.

And, in the end, that was the most important thing. Because no matter how great the treasure, how significant the legacy, what really matters is who you are. And the Tar Society Boys were, and would always be, boys. Boys with an adventurous, brave, and indomitable spirit. Boys who, even when they became kings, never forgot to be boys.

And so, the legend of the Tar Society Boys continues. A legend about boys, adventures, and a lost treasure. A legend that will be told and retold, passed down from generation to generation.

Because, in the end, we are all a bit like the Tar Society Boys. We are all adventurers, dreamers, explorers. We all have a treasure to guard, a story to tell.

And that's what makes life a great adventure. That's what makes each of us unique, special. That's what makes each of us a Tar Society Boy.

So always remember to be brave, to be adventurous, to be curious. Always remember to be a Tar Society Boy. Because, in the end, that's what really matters."

Chapter 8: The Unexpected Rescue

Dawn broke at the ghost castle, the first rays of sun pouring over the broken battlements. Life in the castle had become routine for the Boys of the Tar Society. They had embraced their role as guardians with seriousness and dedication, but even amid the responsibility of caring for the treasure, they still found time to be boys.

On a sunny morning, Boka, the leader, was walking through the magical forest surrounding the castle. He was used to the calm and peace of the place, but something felt different that day. The air was charged with a sense of urgency that he couldn't understand.

Suddenly, he saw a familiar figure approaching. It was Kolnay, the leader of the Redshirts, the old rival of the Tar Society. Boka was immediately on alert. What was Kolnay doing here?

Kolnay looked desperate. His face was pale, and his clothes were dirty and torn. Boka, despite his past disagreements with the Redshirts, felt a twinge in his heart at seeing Kolnay's state.

"The Redshirts need help," said Kolnay, panting. "We... we found another tunnel. A tunnel leading straight into the heart of the city. And... and we're in trouble. Big trouble."

Boka didn't need any more explanations. He immediately gathered the other boys and set off for the city. They arrived just in time to see the chaos. The tunnel the Redshirts had discovered had somehow collapsed, trapping some of them inside.

The Boys of the Tar Society didn't think twice. They started to work, removing stones and earth, shouting for their lost friends. Despite all their past fights and disagreements, at that moment, they were all just boys. Boys who wanted to save their friends.

The Boys of the Tar Society and the Redshirts worked together, each setting aside their differences to help rescue those who were trapped. And after hours of hard work, they succeeded. The trapped Redshirts were rescued, bruised and frightened, but alive.

That day marked a change. The rivalry between the Boys of the Tar Society and the Redshirts now seemed insignificant. They had worked together, saved lives together. They had become friends.

From that day, the Tar Society and the Redshirts became one team. They shared their adventures, their fears, their victories. They learned to trust each other, to respect each other.

And they learned an important lesson. They learned that, no matter how different they may be, in the end, they were all just boys. Boys who loved adventure, who loved freedom. Boys who, when the situation called for it, could unite and become something greater.

The unexpected rescue became a legend among them. A story they would tell their children, and their children would tell theirs. A story of bravery, friendship, and unity.

And so, the legend of the Boys of the Tar Society and the Redshirts continued. A legend that transcended rivalry, that united two groups that had previously seen each other as enemies. A legend that showed everyone that, in the end, we are all just boys. Boys seeking adventure, freedom, friendship.

And that's what makes life a great adventure. That's what makes each of us unique, special. That's what makes each of us a Boy of the Tar Society, a Redshirt.

So, always remember to be brave, to be adventurous, to be a friend. Always remember to be a Boy of the Tar Society, a Redshirt. Because, in the end, that's what really matters."

Chapter 9: The Story of the Castle

The days passed peacefully for the boys, now united as a large family. They had learned a lot since the encounter in the tunnel, and not just about working together. The Tar Society and the Redshirts had turned into true explorers and protectors of the treasure and the castle.

One day, while rummaging through the ancient chambers, Chico, the most restless of the group, found a parchment yellowed by time. It was a letter, dated many centuries ago, written by a certain Sir Edmund, one of the old lords of the castle.

The content of the parchment was fascinating. It revealed the story of the castle and its former occupants. It spoke of battles, treasures, and ancient legends. The boys were amazed by the discoveries.

They learned about the wars the castle had witnessed, about the treasures it had held, and the secrets it still hid. The castle, once a mysterious and slightly frightening structure, now seemed to come alive in their imaginations.

The stories told in the parchment also spoke of a certain White Knight, a noble and brave warrior who had lived in the castle and defended the treasure from various attacks. The White Knight became a legendary figure for the boys. A picture of courage and determination, a hero they aspired to.

As the boys delved deeper into the history of the castle and its former inhabitants, they also became part of it. They began to see themselves as the new guardians of the castle, successors to the White Knight.

Amid the routine of exploring, protecting the treasure, and maintaining the castle, the boys also dedicated themselves to better understanding the history of the place. They even began to reenact some of the battles described in the parchment, taking on the roles of the ancient warriors.

They were no longer just the Boys of the Tar Society or the Redshirts. They were the new White Knights, the defenders of the castle and the treasure.

In every corner of the castle, in every stone, and in every piece of old furniture, they saw the marks of the past. They felt the presence of the old inhabitants, the warriors and kings who had walked the same corridors they now explored.

The castle was no longer just a refuge, it was their home. A home full of history, adventure, and magic.

The castle's story became part of their story. And they were determined to add their own chapters to it.

They were the Boys of the Tar Society, the Redshirts, the White Knights. They were the guardians of the castle and the treasure. They were part of the story. And they were ready to face any adventure that came their way.

And so, the legend of the castle continued. A legend of bravery, friendship, and unity. A legend that, just like the boys', will be passed down from generation to generation.

And that's what makes life a great adventure. That's what makes each of us unique, special. That's what makes each of us a Boy of the Tar Society, a Redshirt, a White Knight.

So, always remember to be brave, to be adventurous, to be a friend. Always remember to be a guardian of the castle and the treasure. Because, in the end, that's what really matters."

Chapter 10: The Boys' Mission

With the history of the castle and the White Knight fresh in their minds, the boys felt a new sense of purpose. Now, they were not just boys having fun and playing in the streets of Budapest. They were the new guardians of the castle and the treasure.

In their hands was the mission to protect the castle from invaders, to take care of the treasure, and most importantly, to perpetuate the history of the place. Each of them felt the weight of responsibility, but also the pride of being entrusted with such a grand mission.

The Tar Society and the Redshirts, once rivals, were now partners in a mission that demanded courage and determination from them. They felt they were living a chapter of an epic story, and each of them played an important role in it.

To fulfill their mission, the boys knew they needed to strengthen the castle. Based on the accounts from the parchment and their own observations, they developed a plan to repair the damaged parts of the castle and reinforce its defenses.

It was hard work, but they faced it with determination and enthusiasm. Each stone they put in place, each wall they fixed, they felt they were adding their own mark to the history of the castle.

Amid the work, they also found time to have fun. After all, they were still boys, full of energy and imagination. They ran through the castle corridors, played hide and seek in the dungeons, and organized knight tournaments in the open fields.

But when the sun went down, and they gathered around the campfire, the seriousness of their mission returned to their minds. They talked about their plans for the castle, about the legends of the White Knight, and about how they were making a difference in the history of the place.

They were no longer just the Boys of the Tar Society or the Redshirts. They were the new guardians of the castle, the new White Knights. And they had a mission to fulfill.

With each passing day, the boys became more united and more committed to the mission. They felt they were doing something important, something that would leave their mark on the world.

They were the new White Knights, the guardians of the castle and the treasure. They were the new generation of heroes, ready to face any challenge that arose. And they were eager to write their own chapter in the castle's history.

And so, the castle, which had once been a refuge for them, was now their home. It was where they lived their greatest adventures, discovered new secrets, and prepared to face the challenges of the future.

They knew that the mission they had ahead would not be easy. There would be dangers, challenges, moments of doubt and fear. But they also knew they were ready to face them. Because they were the new White Knights, the guardians of the castle and the treasure.

And so, the legend of the castle continued, written by the hands and hearts of a group of brave and determined boys. They were the new generation of heroes, ready to leave their mark on the world.

Because in the end, that's what really matters. It doesn't matter the size of the challenge, or how great the adversity. What really matters is the courage to face it, the determination to overcome it, and the friendship that sustains us along the way.

And that's what makes life a great adventure. That's what makes each of us unique, special. That's what makes each of us a Boy of the Tar Society, a Redshirt, a White Knight.

So, always remember to be brave, to be adventurous, to be a friend. Always remember to be a guardian of the castle and the treasure. Because, in the end, that's what really matters."

Chapter 11: The Attack of the Redshirts

The days of peace and hard work at the castle were interrupted when the scouts of the Tar Society Boys spotted a group of red figures in the distance. The Redshirts, who until then were their partners in the mission to protect the castle, seemed to have had a change of heart. Armed with sticks and stones, they marched towards the castle with a determined look on their faces.

The Tar Society Boys prepared for the attack. Although alarmed, they were also determined. They knew that the castle was their home and the treasure their duty. They could not allow it to be taken by others.

As soon as the Redshirts arrived at the foot of the castle, they launched their attack. A rain of stones flew towards the castle walls, and the Redshirts charged the entrances with sticks in hand. The Tar Society Boys took their positions, ready to defend their home.

The ensuing battle was chaotic and fierce. The Tar Society Boys, although outnumbered, fought bravely. They used everything they had at hand - stones, sticks, even their bare hands - to fend off the Redshirts.

But the Redshirts were strong and persistent. They continued to advance, despite the defenses of the Tar Society Boys. With each step they took, the boys' hearts beat faster, and uncertainty about the outcome of the battle grew.

Then, in the midst of the battle, something unexpected happened. One of the Redshirts, who was about to strike one of the boys with his stick, suddenly stopped. He looked at the boy, at the stick in his hand, and then at the castle behind him.

He lowered his stick and stepped back. The other Redshirts, seeing what he had done, also stopped. There was a moment of silence, a moment of indecision, and then the Redshirts began to retreat.

The Tar Society Boys watched, stunned, as the Redshirts moved away. They did not understand what had happened, but they were relieved. They had managed to defend their home.

Later, when the dust settled, they went to the spot where the Redshirt had stopped. There, they found a small metal insignia. It was the same insignia that was engraved on the parchment, the same insignia of the White Knight.

The boys then understood what had happened. The Redshirt had recognized the insignia, had recognized the boys' mission. He realized they were not enemies, but comrades. And he decided that he could not fight against them.

The boys looked at the insignia, then at the castle, and felt relief. They knew they had gone through a significant challenge, but they also knew they had managed to overcome it. And they knew that no matter how difficult the situation was, they would be ready to face it. Because they were the Tar Society Boys, they were the new White Knights, and they were ready to protect the castle and the treasure at all costs."

Chapter 12: Gereb's Betrayal

The days passed peacefully after the unexpected retreat of the Redshirts. The Tar Society Boys continued their efforts to fortify the castle and protect the treasure. However, an atmosphere of mistrust hung over them, a suspicion that was impossible to ignore.

Amid all this, Gereb, one of the Tar Society Boys, was displaying odd behaviors. He kept to himself, avoided group work, and spent long hours alone. The change was so noticeable that the boys began questioning his loyalty.

In the beginning, Gereb was the most enthusiastic among them. He was always on the frontline, always ready to face any challenge. But now, Gereb seemed like a specter of his former self, evasive and silent.

The boys decided to confront him, trying to understand what was happening. But Gereb refused to respond, merely keeping his silence and his empty gaze. The worry among the boys grew, and with it, the suspicion of betrayal.

One night, the boys decided to follow Gereb. He had become increasingly nocturnal, disappearing into the darkness and only returning at dawn. They followed him silently, careful not to be detected.

They followed him to a remote part of the forest, where they found Gereb in a secret meeting with an unknown figure. The figure was hooded and wore a red coat, the unmistakable mark of the Redshirts.

The boys were shocked to see Gereb speaking with the enemy. They felt betrayed, the feeling of trust shattered into pieces. But before they could act, the hooded figure disappeared into the darkness of the forest.

They confronted Gereb, the accusation of betrayal weighing in their voices. Gereb did not deny it, he just looked at them with empty eyes. There were no excuses, nor regret. Only silence.

Gereb's betrayal shook the Tar Society Boys. They felt betrayed, their hearts heavy with the pain of the betrayal. But they also felt strengthened, united in their determination to protect the castle and the treasure.

Gereb was exiled from the castle, left behind as a reminder of the betrayal he had committed. But even with his departure, the suspicion remained. Gereb's betrayal had been a shock to them all, a reminder of the reality of the situation they were in.

The boys continued to protect the castle and the treasure, their hearts heavy, but resolute. They knew that the path ahead was filled with challenges and hardships, but they were ready to face them.

Gereb's betrayal was a hard blow to the Tar Society Boys. But, in a way, it also strengthened them, uniting them even more in their determination to protect what was theirs. Gereb's betrayal taught them a hard, but necessary lesson: not everyone who stands by your side is truly with you.

And so, the boys continued on their journey, their hearts heavy, but full of determination. Gereb's betrayal did not break their spirit, it only fortified it. Because they were the Tar Society Boys, and nothing was going to stop them."

Chapter 13: The Death of István

It was a rainy day, the gray sky reflecting the gloomy mood of the Tar Society Boys. They were more united than ever after Gereb's betrayal, but the atmosphere was still heavy, still marked by distrust. In this tense climate, they received news that would shock them - István was gravely ill.

István, the eldest among them, was the undisputed leader. With his wisdom and courage, he had always guided the group, even in the hardest moments. But now, István was lying in a bed, with a high fever consuming his strength.

The boys gathered around István, their faces reflecting the concern they felt. István, despite his condition, tried to comfort them with a weak smile. He encouraged them to continue, to not let his illness obstruct the mission they had at hand.

The days passed and István did not improve. The fever persisted and his strength diminished day by day. The boys, despite their desperate attempts, felt an increasing helplessness. They wanted to help István, but nothing they did seemed to work.

Until one day, István summoned the boys to his side. He spoke with a weak but firm voice, knowing that time was running out. István asked the boys to continue protecting the castle and the treasure, to not let his death be in vain.

The boys listened, tears running down their faces. They promised István that they would fulfill his last wish, that they would continue to fight, no matter what.

István's death was a tragedy for the Tar Society Boys. They lost not only their leader but also a friend, a brother. The pain of their loss was almost unbearable, but they held onto the promise they made to István.

They refused to allow István's death to be in vain. They would fight, not just for themselves, but also for István. Because they were the Tar Society Boys, and István's death would only strengthen their determination.

Days turned into weeks and weeks turned into months. István's loss still weighed heavily on them, but they remained firm. They continued to protect the castle and the treasure, as they promised István.

And, despite the pain and loss, they found strength in their promise to István. They continued to fight, to face all the challenges that arose in their path. They refused to give up, to allow István's death to be in vain.

István's death was a hard blow to the Tar Society Boys. But it also served as a cruel reminder of life's reality, of its fragility. They learned that life was precious and that every moment should be treasured.

And so, István's memory continued to live in the hearts of the Tar Society Boys. Through their promise to István, they found the strength to carry on, to face all the challenges that arose in their path.

István's death was a tragedy, but also a catalyst. It strengthened the boys' determination, brought them even closer together. They were the Tar Society Boys, and nothing would stop them. They would continue to fight, to protect what was theirs. For István's memory. For the Tar Society."

Chapter 14: The Boys' Escape

The boys felt the weight of István's loss upon them. The castle, which once seemed a place of adventure and mystery, now seemed gloomy and cold. István's smile and laughter no longer echoed through its walls. But they couldn't let themselves be discouraged. They had promised István they would protect the castle and the treasure, and they would not let his death be in vain.

Over time, the Redshirts became increasingly audacious in their attacks. Each day, the danger moved closer and closer to the castle. The boys knew they had to do something, and quickly.

That's when they decided. They would flee from the castle and take the treasure with them. They knew it would be a difficult task, but they also knew it was the only way to fulfill the promise they made to István.

The night they chose for their escape was cold and starry. They packed the treasure carefully into bags and prepared to leave. The shadows of the night enveloped them, and the boys, with heavy hearts, left the castle behind.

The journey was not easy. They had to walk through dense forests and climb steep hills, always careful not to be seen by the Redshirts. But the boys were strong and determined. They kept going, despite the exhaustion and cold.

Along the way, the boys remembered István. They remembered his courage, his smile, his determination. Each step they took, they took for him.

After days of travel, they finally found a safe place to rest. It was a small valley, hidden between tall mountains and dense forests. There, they rested and regained their strength.

The boys spent the next day exploring the valley, looking for a safe place to hide the treasure. Eventually, they found a small cave, hidden behind a waterfall. It was the perfect place.

The boys took the treasure to the cave and carefully hid it. Then, with a heavy heart, they looked out over the valley. They knew their journey was not over. They had to find a new home, far from the Redshirts.

As time passed, the boys began to adapt to their new life. They learned to survive in nature, to hunt and fish. Despite the hardships, they never forgot their promise to István. They continued to fight, to protect what was theirs.

The escape from the castle had been difficult, but the boys were determined. They knew they had a mission to fulfill, a promise to keep. They were the Tar Society Boys, and nothing would stop them. They would continue to fight, for István's memory, for the treasure, for the castle. They would never give up."

Chapter 15: The Tunnel Collapse

Time had passed since the boys had left the castle and found a new refuge in the valley. The seasons changed, the cold of winter gave way to the heat of summer, but the memory of István remained strong in their hearts.

The boys had started to explore more of the area around their refuge, in search of resources and escape routes in case the Redshirts found them. It was during one of these explorations that they discovered a subterranean passage that seemed to be a tunnel.

The tunnel was narrow and dark, but seemed safe enough to explore. The boys decided they should investigate it, to see if it led to somewhere useful or could serve as an escape route in case of emergency.

Equipped with lanterns, the boys ventured into the tunnel. The darkness was oppressive, but their curiosity was stronger. They advanced slowly, illuminating the path with their lanterns.

After some time, they began to hear a strange noise coming from the end of the tunnel. It was a low, constant sound, as if something was moving. The boys stopped and listened, trying to identify what it was.

That's when it happened. Without warning, the tunnel started to shake. Rocks and earth began to fall from the ceiling. The boys realized what was happening and started running back towards the entrance.

They had barely begun to run when the tunnel collapsed behind them. The sound was deafening, and the dust raised by the collapse made it nearly impossible to see.

The boys ran as fast as they could, but the collapse was closing in. Rocks fell around them, the dust stung their eyes, and the darkness seemed to grow closer and closer.

That's when Boka, the fastest of them all, reached the entrance of the tunnel. He turned around and extended his hand to the others, trying to help them out. One by one, the boys managed to escape the collapsing tunnel.

Finally, they were all outside, panting and covered in dirt. They looked back at the tunnel that was now just a pile of rocks and earth.

Despite the scare, the boys were relieved. They had escaped the tunnel collapse without a scratch. They hugged each other and laughed, relieved to be safe.

But the laughter soon gave way to worry. The tunnel that could have served as an escape route was now blocked. They would have to find another way to escape if the Redshirts found them.

They spent the rest of the day exploring the area around the valley, but found no other passages or tunnels. The tunnel collapse had been a hard blow, but the boys knew they couldn't afford to give up.

As the sun set, they returned to their refuge, determined to find a new escape route. They knew the fight was far from over. They had to carry on, for István's memory, for the treasure, for the castle. They would never give up."

Chapter 16: The Search for an Exit

The next day, the boys woke up early. The sun was still rising, painting the sky with hues of pink and orange, but the boys were already on their feet, ready to start the search for a new exit.

After a quick breakfast, they split into groups of two and three, each with a different direction to explore. They had a plan and were determined to carry it out.

Boka and Ernő headed north, towards the heart of the forest. They moved cautiously, their eyes alert for any sign of a path or something that could be useful for their escape.

Árpád and Gergely, on the other hand, went west, towards the hills. They knew the climb would be tough, but they hoped to find something up there that could help them.

Finally, the Kolnay and Weisz brothers went south, towards the river. They had hopes of finding a bridge or something that could allow them to cross the river undetected.

The boys spent the entire day exploring, moving through the forest, climbing hills, and following the course of the river. But no matter how much they searched, they found nothing that could help them.

At the end of the day, they returned to their refuge, tired and discouraged. But they did not give up. They knew the search would be hard, but they were determined to find an exit.

That night, they sat around the campfire, discussing their findings of the day. They talked about the paths they had taken, the things they had seen, and the possibilities each direction offered.

Despite the discouragement, there was a sense of determination among them. They knew the task was tough, but they were willing to face the challenge. They had a mission to fulfill and they would not give up.

The next day, they resumed the search. They explored new areas, sought new paths, and kept the hope of finding an exit. Each day brought new challenges, but also new possibilities.

Days turned into weeks, and weeks into months. The boys grew thinner and more tired, but they never gave up. They kept searching, exploring, looking for an exit.

And, finally, after months of searching, they found something. It was a small path, hidden among the trees, that seemed to lead out of the valley. It was narrow and hard to see, but it was there.

The boys were thrilled. They had found an exit. They had found hope.

That night, they celebrated. They laughed, told stories, and made plans for the future. They knew they still had a long way ahead, but for the first time in months, they had hope.

The next day, they began to prepare for the journey. They gathered supplies, studied the path, and made plans for the future.

And, as the sun rose the following day, they set off. They left the valley behind, they left the castle and the forest and the tunnel. They were going home.

The path was tough and the journey long, but they didn't care. They had found an exit. They were going home.

And, as they walked, the boys looked back at the valley and the castle and the forest. They looked at the place that had been their prison, their refuge, and their home. They looked back and smiled, knowing they had found an exit.

And with that, they moved forward, determined to return home, determined to win. Because they were the Paul Street Boys, and nothing would stop them."

Chapter 17: The Temporary Alliance

The Paul Street Boys were on their way home. Their joy, however, was interrupted when, upon turning a corner, they came face-to-face with a familiar face. It was Tibor Geréb, the traitor who had delivered István to the Redshirts.

Tibor's expression, however, was not one of triumph, but of fear and desperation. He had also escaped from the castle, but was lost and without supplies. Seeing the boys, a spark of hope ignited in his eyes.

The boys looked at Geréb with suspicion, their memories of his betrayal still fresh. However, Árpád, always the most practical, quickly assessed the situation. "We need him," he said, "He knows the way back to Budapest."

Árpád's argument did not please everyone, but they eventually agreed to form a temporary alliance with Geréb. They would help him in exchange for guidance. Geréb, seeing the alternative, accepted the offer.

The march to Budapest was tough. The terrain was rough and wild, and Geréb, despite everything, was not a reliable guide. They often got lost, which prolonged their journey and tested their patience.

Despite this, the boys remained steadfast. Their determination was fueled by the memory of István and the desire to return to the safety of their homes. No matter what happened, they would keep moving forward.

Geréb, for his part, was clearly uncomfortable with the situation. He avoided looking at the boys, preferring to focus on the task of guiding them. He seemed to understand the depth of his betrayal and the resentment it caused.

However, as the journey progressed, something strange happened. Geréb, perhaps motivated by necessity, began to open up to the boys. He shared stories of his childhood and explained, albeit reluctantly, why he had joined the Redshirts.

The revelation shocked the boys, but it also helped them understand Geréb. He was a boy who had gotten lost, who had made the wrong choices out of fear and desperation. It didn't justify his actions, but it gave them a different perspective.

Over time, the hostility between Geréb and the boys began to diminish. They weren't friends, but there was a tacit understanding between them. They were survivors, bound together by circumstances beyond their control.

Finally, after weeks of travel, they arrived at the outskirts of Budapest. The city was changed, marked by the effects of the war, but still recognizable. The boys felt a mix of relief and sadness. They were home, but at what cost?

Geréb stopped at the edge of the city, refusing to go any further. "This is the end of the line for me," he said, his gaze fixed on the city. The boys understood. Budapest had been the city that had betrayed him; he couldn't go back.

So, with a silent nod, Geréb turned and walked away. The Paul Street Boys watched him go, a strange feeling of gratitude in their hearts. He had betrayed one of them, but in the end, he had also helped to bring them home.

As they entered Budapest, they felt flooded with a wave of emotions. The city had changed, but it was still their city. They were finally home.

As they looked at the city before them, the Paul Street Boys made a silent pact. They would honor the memory of István. They would rebuild what had been destroyed. They would make Budapest the city they once loved.

And, with that determination in their hearts, they marched into the future, ready to face whatever was ahead. Because they were the Paul Street Boys, and nothing would stop them."

Chapter 18: The Light at the End of the Tunnel

The Paul Street Boys were home, but Budapest was no longer the same. The city was scarred by war, its once bustling streets now empty and silent. However, the boys were not discouraged; they were determined to bring life back to their beloved city.

Their first task was to rebuild their headquarters, the lot they had been stripped of by the Redshirts. It was a strenuous task, but the boys worked with purpose. Each stone laid, each nail hammered was a step towards the future they desired.

As they worked, they couldn't help but notice the solitary figure of Tibor Geréb watching them from a distance. He didn't interfere, just observed. There was something in his posture, in his silence, that suggested a change. Tibor Geréb was different.

Days passed and the headquarters began to take shape. One morning, as the boys were working, Tibor Geréb approached. He was nervous, his hands slightly shaking. In a soft voice, he offered his help.

The boys were surprised. They watched Geréb, trying to understand his intentions. Árpád, however, saw something else. He saw a lost boy trying to redeem himself. And with a nod, he accepted Geréb's help.

Together, they worked on rebuilding the headquarters. It was a joint effort, an alliance formed not out of friendship, but out of understanding and respect. And gradually, the scars of war began to fade, replaced by signs of life and hope.

Finally, the day arrived when the Paul Street Boys' headquarters was complete. Looking at their creation, the boys felt a mix of pride and relief. They had done it. They had rebuilt their home.

On that day, they held a small ceremony, not only to celebrate the completion of the headquarters, but also to honor the memory of István. They raised a flag atop the building, the same flag István always carried with him. It was a moment of silence, a moment of respect and remembrance.

As the flag fluttered in the wind, the boys turned their gaze towards the future. They had overcome many obstacles, but they knew there were still many challenges ahead. However, they were ready. They were determined.

And so, they prepared for the next step, to rebuild Budapest, to make it again the city they loved. And as they worked, one thing became clear. They were the Paul Street Boys, and they had found the light at the end of the tunnel."

Chapter 19: The Final Surprise

There was a palpable energy on Paul Street that morning. The Boys were gathered at their newly rebuilt headquarters, each dressed in their Sunday best. They looked at each other with an expectant glint in their eyes. They were awaiting a surprise.

Bokor led the boys to the center of Paul Street, where a crowd was gathering. It was not just the boys' parents, but also neighbors and friends, all with ear-to-ear smiles. In the middle of the crowd, there was a large box covered with a thick cloth.

Bokor raised his hand to silence the crowd and pointed to the box. With a nod, Weisz and Csele grabbed the corners of the cloth and pulled it away, revealing what was hidden underneath.

There it was, gleaming in the sunlight, a brand new bronze plaque. On it were engraved the words: "Paul Street Boys' Playground." There was also an inscription further down, a tribute to István: "In memory of our brave and loyal friend, István Török."

The Paul Street Boys' eyes filled with tears. They looked at each other and then at the plaque, feeling a mixture of emotions. Joy, sadness, longing, and above all, gratitude.

Árpád stepped forward and, with a choked voice, thanked everyone present. He promised that they would honor István's memory by playing fair and bravely, exactly as he would have wished.

The crowd clapped as the boys retrieved a soccer ball from the box. Bokor placed the ball in the middle of the newly refurbished field, and the boys lined up for the kickoff.

For a moment, they just stood there, looking at the ball. Then, without a word, Bokor stepped forward and kicked the ball. The game had begun.

It was more than a game. It was a tribute to their fallen friend and a celebration of their childhood, a remembrance of the frolics and disputes of Paul Street. With each kick, each goal, they felt István's presence among them.

Finally, as the sun began to set, the game came to an end. The Paul Street Boys gathered in the middle of the field, huddled together, laughing and crying. They had been through so many challenges, so many losses and betrayals. But they were here. They were still the Paul Street Boys.

They looked at the plaque one last time before leaving the field. In the quiet of the night, they could almost hear István's laughter, the echo of his footsteps running across the field.

The boys dispersed, each heading back to their homes. But they all knew that no matter where they went, there would always be a place for them on Paul Street. They would always be the Paul Street Boys.

As Paul Street fell asleep, the bronze plaque glowed in the moonlight. A silent tribute to bravery, loyalty, and friendship. To the struggles and victories of the Paul Street Boys. And to the memory of the boy who had fought and died to protect them.

And so, despite all the hardships and challenges, the Paul Street Boys found their final surprise. They had lost a friend, but gained an everlasting memory. A memory that would inspire and guide them for the rest of their lives.

And somewhere, István smiled, knowing that his friends were safe, that Paul Street was safe. And that the Paul Street Boys, his friends, his brothers, would continue to fight and play, to live and laugh, always honoring his memory.

In the end, that was the real surprise: the strength of friendship, the courage in the face of adversity, and the joy of being young. That was the real story of the Paul Street Boys. And that story, like the memory of István, would live forever."

Chapter 20: The Return to the Grund

It was a new day on Paul Street. The Boys, now a little older, a little wiser, but still the same, gathered at the grund. The place had been cleaned and refurbished, a playground gleaming in the sunlight.

Bokor, as always, was the first to arrive. With a slight smile on his face, he looked around the familiar grund. Each piece of the place brought back memories - some good, some painful, but all precious.

Soon, the other boys started to arrive. They greeted each other and spread out over the grund, exploring and rediscovering every corner. Each of them, in their own way, feeling the nostalgia and comfort of that cherished place.

It was like coming home after a long journey. Despite everything they had been through, the grund was still theirs. They had changed, but the grund remained the same, a constant landmark in their lives.

As they explored, they found the tree where there had once been a rope hanging. Now, however, a swing had been placed there. It was new, but fit in perfectly. An addition that only added to the beauty of the grund.

Bokor was the first to sit on the swing. He looked at the other boys and smiled. They joined him, laughing and playing as they did in the old days.

Árpád, in turn, discovered something interesting. The old well, which used to be just an empty hole, was now filled with clean water. He leaned down to grab some of the water, which sparkled in the sunlight.

With a laugh, he threw a handful of water at the other boys, prompting an impromptu water war. They ran and hid, throwing water at each other, laughing and having fun like never before.

But, while they played, a shadow passed over the grund. It was a brief moment, just a blink of an eye, but it made the boys stop and look up. There, in the sky, flew a red bird, its wings shining in the sun.

The boys looked at each other, smiles spreading across their faces. It was a sign. They knew it. István was there with them, joining in the play, the laughter, the joy. He would never leave them, they knew.

With renewed energy, they returned to their games. They played until the sun went down, until the last ray of light disappeared over the horizon. And when they finally went home, each of them carried the certainty that they would always be united, they would always be the Paul Street Boys.

That day, they discovered that no matter how far you go, or how tough the journey, there is always a way back home. To the grund, to Paul Street, to childhood. To the friends you made, the memories you created, and the challenges you overcame.

The return to the grund was more than just a physical return. It was a return to innocence, to joy, to friendship. It was a return to childhood and everything it represented.

And so, the grund became once again the sanctuary of the Paul Street Boys. A fortress against the outside world, a place of laughter and joy, a monument to courage and loyalty. And, above all, a reminder of the friend they had lost, but whose spirit would live forever in their hearts.

The Paul Street Boys returned to the grund. And, somehow, it seemed like they had never left. The street was silent, the grund was empty, but the memories were still there, as vivid as ever.

And so, the Paul Street Boys continued to live and laugh, to play and dream. Always together, always loyal, always the Paul Street Boys. And, deep down, they knew it would always be that way. No matter where life took them, they would always return to the grund, always come back home.

And so ends the story of the Paul Street Boys. A story of friendship and courage, of loyalty and loss. A story that, like the boys who starred in it, will never be forgotten. Because, in the end, they will always be the Paul Street Boys. They will always be the grund. And the grund will always be theirs."

Made in the USA
Las Vegas, NV
16 December 2024